A ROOKIE READER

HOT ROD HARRY

By Catherine Petrie

Illustrations by Paul Sharp

Prepared under the direction of Robert Hillerich, Ph.D.

CHILDRENS PRESS ™

CHICAGO

For Joshua

Library of Congress Cataloging in Publication Data

Petrie, Catherine.
  Hot Rod Harry.

  (A Rookie reader)
  Summary: Hot Rod Harry rides so fast on his
bike he almost seems to fly like a bird or a jet.
  [1. Bicycles and bicycling—Fiction]
I. Sharp, Paul (Paul W.), ill.   II. Title.
III. Series.
PZ7.P44677Ho   [E]   81-15549
ISBN 0-516-03493-6   AACR2

Hot Rod Harry rides a bike.

Zoom! Zoom!

To be fast is what he likes.

8

9

10

He rides fast.

Never slow.

13

Look at Hot Rod Harry go!

15

He's a bird who can fly.

He's a jet in the sky.

Hot Rod Harry on his bike.

To be fast is what he likes.

He rides fast.

Never slow.

Look at Hot Rod Harry go!

WORD LIST

		never
a	he	on
at	he's	rides
be	his	slow
bike	Hot Rod Harry	the
bird	in	to
can	is	sky
fast	jet	what
fly	likes	who
go	look	zoom

About the Author

Catherine Petrie is a reading specialist with a Master of Science degree in Reading. She has been teaching reading in the public school system for the past ten years. Her experience as a teacher has made her aware of the lack of material currently available for the very young reader. Her creative use of a limited vocabulary based on high-frequency sight words, combined with frequent repetition and rhyming word families, provide the beginning reader with a positive independent reading experience. *Hot Rod Harry, Sandbox Betty,* and *Joshua James Likes Trucks* are her first published beginning readers.

About the Artist

Paul Sharp graduated from the Art Institute of Pittsburgh.
He has worked for the Curtis Publishing Company as Art Director of Child Life magazine.
At the present time he works as a free-lance artist at his home in Indianapolis, Indiana.